Scholastic's
The Magic School Bus
SHOWS AND TELLS
A Book About Archaeology

™

P.S. 145 LIBRARY

SCHOLASTIC INC.
New York   Toronto   London   Auckland   Sydney

From an episode of the animated TV series
produced by Scholastic Productions, Inc.
Based on *The Magic School Bus* books
written by Joanna Cole and illustrated by Bruce Degen

TV tie-in adaptation by Jackie Posner and illustrated by John Speirs.
TV script written by John May.

ISBN 0-590-92242-4

12 11   2/0

Printed in the U.S.A.   **23**

First Scholastic printing, February 1997

Our class really digs having Ms. Frizzle for a teacher —
she makes every day fun! And today was no different.
It all started at the International Show and Tell
Competition. Our class was to show Arnold's rare rock
collection. The only problem was, Arnold was nowhere
to be found!

"Where is Arnold?" cried Phoebe, nervously looking at her watch. "The show's about to start!"

"I don't know what you're worried about," said Dorothy Ann. "*I'm* the one who has to go out there and tell them what we have!"

If Arnold doesn't get here soon, we'll be disqualified!

We were beginning to panic when in raced Arnold.
"Y-you guys are really going to thank me!" he said,
gasping for air.

"Where's your rock collection?" asked Dorothy Ann.

"At home. I brought this instead," said Arnold. He
pulled out of his bag a strange-looking hoop with a
colorful net attached. "Is this *great* or *what*?"

"What is it?" asked Tim.

"I don't know," replied Arnold. "I'm just the 'Show' part. Dorothy Ann is the 'Tell' part."

Dorothy Ann looked at the hoop carefully. She turned it over and over in her hands. "I've spent the last two weeks digging up rock information. I don't have a clue what this thing is!" she finally exclaimed.

There was no time for Arnold to go home and get his rocks. But we couldn't enter the competition with this hoop. We weren't even sure what it was!

Suddenly Ms. Frizzle showed up. "You're just in time," Dorothy Ann told her. "Arnold brought this weird hoop for Show and Tell, but nobody knows what it is!"

"Well, as my nephew Conrad always says, 'When in doubt, figure it out!'" Ms. Frizzle said.

The first thing we figured out was that Arnold found the hoop in a trunk that belonged to his great-aunt, the famous archaeologist known as Arizona Joan.

"When I was little," said Arnold, "Aunt Joan used to tell me stories about what she did as an archaeologist — how she searched for things that were left behind by people a long time ago. She'd figure out how people lived based on the stuff she found."

"So, did she ever tell you what this was?" asked Wanda.

"She never figured it out," replied Arnold. "But I do have this journal of her adventures."

"Maybe there are some clues in here," said Dorothy Ann, taking the journal from Arnold.

When you think like an archaeologist, clues are news!

Just then, Ms. Frizzle got that gleam in her eyes. "To the bus, class!" she called.

"Wait," cried Arnold. "If you're talking about a field trip, we can't go now! What about the show? We're about to go on!"

Dorothy Ann turned to Arnold. "Unless I can TELL everybody what your Aunt Joan found, there is no SHOW!" she shouted.

Ms. Frizzle gave Arnold a two-way Show and Tell-evision so he could hear and see us at all times.

"So how do we figure out what this hoop is for if the people who used it aren't around to tell us?" Wanda asked Ms. Frizzle as we boarded the bus.

Ms. Frizzle took the hoop from Wanda. "Archaeologists call something like this an artifact," she said.

"So an artifact is anything made by people who lived a long time ago?" Tim asked.

"Exactly, Tim!" Ms. Frizzle said.

But we still couldn't figure out *why* someone made the hoop. Then Ms. Frizzle told us that we'd have to *guess* the reason!

"Archaeologists put clues together and make a guess," Ms. Frizzle explained. "They call that guess a hypothesis."

A hypothesis — I could have guessed that!

We put together our clues. One: The hoop was made of wood. Two: The hoop was strong. Ralphie guessed it was some sort of a war thing—like a shield. But Tim thought it was a net.

"Okay, okay," said Dorothy Ann. "So we have two good guesses—now, what . . . ?" But before she could finish, the Friz turned the bus into a lab.

"Welcome to the Suppose-a-Tron, where all your guesses will be tested," Ms. Frizzle said.

An artifact is a key to the past.

"Now, if an archaeologist is going to try out an artifact, the first thing he or she does is make a *copy* of that artifact," Ms. Frizzle said. She made a copy and gave the original artifact to Liz to bring back to Arnold. Then we joined Ms. Frizzle at the large computer screen.

"Now, we know the hoop was made long ago," began Ms. Frizzle. "But what else do we know?"

"It says here that it was found near Fort Walkerville," said Dorothy Ann, looking at Arizona Joan's journal.

As the Friz entered this information, a map of Walkerville appeared on the screen.

"We know there had to be trees, since it's made of wood!" continued Ralphie. And with that, some trees sprouted up on the screen.

"And there had to be people living there! Somebody must have made it!" exclaimed Tim.

Dorothy Ann looked in the journal again. "Arizona Joan writes about hunters and farmers," she said.

"So maybe we can suppose that the people there sometimes fought over territory," guessed Ralphie.

Ralphie's guess was good, but we didn't know how to find out whether or not his guess was right.

Then a smile crossed Ms. Frizzle's face. We had a feeling something was about to happen—and we were right! One by one, we were tossed *into* the computer screen!

I think we're about to test our hypothesis!

Wahooooo!!!!

Suddenly we found ourselves in the place we had "supposed." The Suppose-a-Tron had taken what we knew, added our guess, and created a "what-if" world. As we looked around our what-if world, all we could see was a tribe of angry-looking people.

"We programmed them for a fight," Ms. Frizzle reminded us. "Better get your shield ready to test that hypothesis!" she shouted to Ralphie.

Running for cover, we watched as an arrow flew right through the hoop's webbing— *TWANG!*—and into a tree— *THUNK!*

"So much for your hypothesis," we yelled to Ralphie as we jumped back through the computer screen to safety.

"Man. That was *close*!" exclaimed Ralphie.

We were just catching our breath when Arnold's voice came through Ms. Frizzle's Tell-evision.

"Attention, class. Come in, class!! You guys know what time it is?" he cried. "We go on stage *any minute now*!"

"We're working on it!" replied Carlos. "But we can tell you it's NOT a war thing."

This hoop probably *wasn't* a war thing....

"It says here that Arizona Joan found remains of canoes near where she found the hoop," noted Wanda, her nose in the journal.

Then Tim picked up the hoop. "Look at this webbing!" he said. "It makes the hoop perfect for grabbing and scooping things. I guessed it was a net, so now I say it's a fish net!"

Ms. Frizzle entered the guess into the Suppose-a-Tron. "C'mon, class, let's make a splash!" she said. Then she dove into the screen. We were a little worried, but we followed her. *Splash! Splash! Splash!*

Paddling downstream, we noticed that the water was full of fish. But every time Tim tried to catch fish with the hoop, they would just slip through the net or swim around it.

"Too bad you can't catch one!" Dorothy Ann said.

Just then, Ms. Frizzle pointed out that we were heading straight for the rapids.

Meanwhile, back at the Show and Tell competition, Arnold turned on his Tell-evision to see us shooting down the rapids. "I can't believe this is happening! I go on any minute now!" he cried. But Liz wasn't worried. She was busy playing, throwing Cheesie Wheesies through the rolling hoop.

Quit playing! This is serious business!

We made it through the rapids safely. But we still hadn't figured out what the hoop was.

Then Keesha picked up the hoop. "When you think about it," she said, "why would they give this hoop all these beautiful colors if they were just going to stick it in the water?"

"So, based on that observation, Keesha, what would *you* say it is?" Ms. Frizzle asked.

"A hat!" she answered.

Dorothy Ann agreed that the hoop could have been a hat. "It says in the journal that Joan found shells and beads that people used to decorate their clothing."

So we guessed that the hat was worn as part of a dance celebration and put our hypothesis to the test. We added dancers, drums, and nighttime to the Suppose-a-Tron.

Before we knew it, we were dancing at a harvest celebration.

"Don't you just love to dance!" sang Keesha as she struggled to keep the hat on her head.

The more Keesha danced, the more the hoop slipped off
her head. "There's no way to keep this hat on," she cried.
"No bands, no ties, no straps . . ."

"And there are no marks on the rim to show where
they could have been," noticed Phoebe.

It looked as if Keesha's hypothesis was wrong.

We were starting to think we'd never figure it out! But
Ms. Frizzle wasn't worried. "I bet my bottom buttons
there are more hypotheses where that one came from!"
she said.

Where'd you get those arrows?

Back at the bus we called Arnold through the
Tell-evision. "Come in, Arnold," we said.

"Dorothy Ann," Arnold said, "what's taking . . ."

"Was there anything else in the bag besides the hoop?"
D.A. asked, interrupting him.

We watched on the screen as Arnold pulled stuff out of
the bag. Some baby pictures, booties, a pacifier, and
suddenly . . . some arrows!

The arrow tips looked dull, and seemed to be decorated just like the hoop. We guessed that the arrows and the hoop went together. But *how*, we wondered.

Suddenly Dorothy Ann realized that the arrows would probably fit through the holes in the hoop's net. "I need one of those arrows!" she exclaimed.

And with that she raced to the auditorium. She grabbed an arrow from Arnold and zoomed back to the lab.

"You're leaving me alone again?" Arnold called after Dorothy Ann. Suddenly he heard our school being announced. "Join me in welcoming the contestant from Walker Elementary School," the announcer said.

Arnold felt sick. "Um. Hi . . ." he said into the microphone. "This is . . . this is . . . an artifact — something from long ago. And from objects like this, we can figure out how people lived their lives — if you know how to read the clues," he continued.

Back at the lab, the Friz made copies of the arrows while Dorothy Ann added information to the Suppose-a-Tron. Before we knew it, we were following Dorothy Ann through the screen into a Hoops and Arrows competition.

"What's going on?" we asked.

"Don't you get it?" responded Dorothy Ann. "What's round, different colors, and goes with something pointy?" she asked excitedly.

"A dartboard!" exclaimed Wanda.

"So maybe our artifact was a game," suggested Phoebe. "And maybe you have to get the arrow through the holes!"

This sounded good to us. Even long ago, people needed to have fun.

Then we noticed that the rim of the hoop was worn down. We guessed that the hoop didn't stay still like a dartboard. Instead, maybe the hoop was rolled along the ground while other people tried to throw their arrows through it.

Let's play Hoops and Arrows!

We were having so much fun playing Hoops and Arrows that we forgot all about poor Arnold.

But Arnold was busy talking to the audience. He was telling them that the hoop might be a shield.

"Ooooh!" cried the audience.

"Well, actually," said Arnold, lifting the hoop to his face, "it would be kind of useless because arrows could go right through the holes . . ."

"Oh," sighed the crowd.

"Um," Arnold continued. He knew he had to keep the audience's attention. "Pretend you're paddling along a river, trying to catch fish. You sweep the water," he said as he pretended to be catching fish with the hoop. "Then realize you better get a paddle that doesn't leak!"

Arnold's heart was pounding. "Imagine you're at a ceremony," he told the audience. "The fire roars, the drummers pound, the dancers sway . . . and then . . ."

"WHAAAT???!" cried the audience.

"You . . . you wonder why you brought this hat because there's no way it will stay on your head when you dance," sighed Arnold as the hoop rolled off the stage. The audience groaned.

But as he chased the rolling hoop, he suddenly figured it out!

"Ladies and gentlemen," Arnold announced, "believe it or not, this artifact is something kids know really well . . . it's a game! The object of the game was probably to get the arrows through the rolling hoop!"

"You see," Arnold told the audience, "this is only a *hypothesis*—a good guess. But the things left behind by people who lived long ago, like this hoop, give us clues about how they lived. And it's up to archaeologists like us to fit the clues together."

The audience clapped loudly for Arnold and stood on their feet.

We ran into the auditorium just as Arnold was being handed the top prize. He bowed and said, "This award doesn't belong to me alone, it belongs to all my classmates at Walker Elementary. Thank you!"

Letters from Our Readers

(Editor's note: They will help you tell what is real and what is make-believe in this story.)

Dear Editor:
It's too bad real archaeologists can't have something like that Suppose-a-Tron. If there was such a thing, anybody could be an archaeologist!
Your Friend,
A Supposer

Dear Supposer,
Even though there is no such thing as a Suppose-a-Tron, we made one up for the story because archaeologists think the way the Suppose-a-Tron works.
The Editor

Dear Editor,
If that hoop was really made of wood, I doubt it would have survived all those years.
Signed,
You Can't Fool Me!

Dear You Can't Fool Me!
You're right! Wood and clothing are the first things to rot away. That's why most ancient artifacts that are still around are things made of stone or pottery or metal.
Good catch!
The Editor

A Note to Kids, Teachers, and Parents

Archaeologists figure out how people lived long ago by collecting and studying artifacts. Artifacts are left-behind objects like pieces of buildings, tools, even toys or games like the Hoops and Arrows game in this book. Buried or hidden away for centuries, artifacts are often our only link to life in the past.

Archaeologists gather data, or information, by digging, chipping, and brushing away layers of soil. They must keep careful records of every artifact they find, including exactly where they found it and how deep it was buried and what shape it's in. From this information, archaeologists can guess the age of the artifact. Even the tiniest artifact may give a clue about how people lived.

Usually one artifact is not enough to make a good guess about life in the past. Just like pieces of a jigsaw puzzle, archaeologists need to find many artifacts in order to fit their clues together.

Ms. Frizzle